PiRATE
Blunderbeard
WORST. MOVIE. EVER.

Join Pirate Blunderbeard on more adventures:

Pirate Blunderbeard
WORST. PIRATE. EVER.

Pirate Blunderbeard
WORST. HOLIDAY. EVER.

Pirate Blunderbeard
WORST. MISSION. EVER.

Pirate Blunderbeard
WORST. MOVIE. EVER.

PiRATE
Blunderbeard

WORST. MOVIE. EVER.

AMY SPARKES & BEN CORT

HarperCollins *Children's Books*

Mum

Blackbeard

Blunderbeard

Barber Rossa

Pirate Pete

Captain Chomp

Boris

Redruth

Captain Hoy

Jolly Roger

First published in Great Britain by
HarperCollins *Children's Books* in 2018
HarperCollins *Children's Books* is a division of HarperCollins*Publisher*s Ltd,
HarperCollins Publishers, 1 London Bridge Street, London SE1 9GF

The HarperCollins website address is
www.harpercollins.co.uk

1

ISBN 978–0–00–820195–1

Printed and bound in England by CPI Group (UK) Ltd, Croydon, CR0 4YY

*For Jonah and Megan, who have been
with Blunders from the beginning.
#TeamFireBreathingChickens*

*Amy Sparkes is donating a percentage of
her royalties to ICP Support, aiming for
every ICP baby to be born safely.*

*Reg. charity no. 1146449
www.icpsupport.org*

JANUARY 1ST

Hellooooo, Crossbones Island! I am BACK!
I've been away a whole year with Grandpa
and my cousin Redruth, exploring the
Seven Seas, capturing ships from fearsome
pirates and rescuing my chicken, Boris,
from various epic disasters.

But now Grandpa has gone off to write his new book, *Proper Pirating for Beginners: Volume 3*. And I'm stuck here.

After a life of danger and adventure, this year is probably going to be really dull just hanging around on the island, but here are my New Year's resolutions:

1. Prove to my big brother Blackbeard once and for all that I am NOT a waste of space

2. Teach Boris a special new skill

3. Do something awesome and make it into *Pirate Monthly* — well, why not?

4. Find an ice-cream boat and get an ice cream!

5. Find a way to get rid of Redruth

FEBRUARY 10TH

Booked Boris in for some karate lessons. It was that or ballet. You never know, karate may be a useful skill.

Wonder what *I'll* do this year?

Nothing ever happens on Crossbones Island.

Nothing.

Ever.

FEBRUARY 28TH

I can't believe what's happening this year!

THIS is amazing!

THIS is going to

change my life!

4

Jolly Roger

PRODUCTIONS PRESENTS:
The Perfect Life of Pirates: THE MOVIE

Amazing, Golden Eyepatch Award-winning actor and director Jolly Roger will be directing *PLOP: The Movie* on Crossbones Island this year.

New cast and crew members required. (Jolly sent the last ones on an all-expenses-paid vacation to his private island to celebrate him winning the Golden Eyepatch Award. It was only after they left that he realised he had no one to make the new film.)

PUBLIC MEETING ABOUT THE FILM:
APRIL 1ST, The Barrel Theatre

AUDITIONS: JUNE 1ST, The Barrel Theatre

Wow! Jolly Roger! He's been in all my favourite pirate movies, like *Feather Island* and *Yo Ho Ho and a Bottle of Prune Juice Because We Ran Out of Everything Else*. And he's really good. He won last year's fabulous Golden Eyepatch Award for Best Actor! THIS is the start of something big! I can feel it in my belly.

Oh, wait. No, that's just yesterday's leftover squid curry . . . Back in a bit!

To-do List:

1. Buy haddock to cook fish and chips for lunch

2. Public meeting 10am, The Barrel Theatre!

Can't believe I'm going to see Jolly Roger face to face!

11am

The Barrel Theatre is amazing – shaped round like a barrel, with wooden walls and a stage at the back. The crowd went wild

when Jolly Roger appeared. It was brilliant
to see him in real life! People threw flowers
at his feet. I didn't think to bring any so
I threw the haddock I bought instead.

It would have been fine if it hadn't knocked Jolly's hat off (whoops). All the pirates in the audience gasped but Jolly just laughed (phew).

Then Jolly made an exciting speech –
exciting as a triple-chocolate cupcake with
double-chocolate sparkly bits on top and
hidden chocolate inside!

I scribbled it all down so I wouldn't forget:
"Friends, pirates, ocean-folk, lend me
your ears! For I have the most excellent
news! I, Jolly Roger, award-winning

actor and director, winner of the amazing Golden Eyepatch for Best Actor at the last ceremony for PANTS (Pirate Actors, Newcomers and Talented Stars), will be producing my latest fabulous film, *The Perfect Life of Pirates: The Movie,* also known as *PLOP: The Movie,* on this very island!"

(YEEEEEEEEEEEK!!!!!)

"The movie is, of course, all about how my magnificent career began when I was a child, and how I became THE most famous actor to sail the Seven Seas! The parts available are ..."

THE AWARD-WINNING ACTOR JOLLY ROGER (AS A CHILD)

THE AWARD-WINNING CANNONBALL-HURLER POLLY ROGER (JOLLY'S SISTER, AS A CHILD)

THE DASTARDLY CAPTAIN CROOK (ARCH-ENEMY AND EVIL PIRATE GENIUS, AS A CHILD)

CARROT THE PARROT (JOLLY'S BELOVED CHILDHOOD PET)

MOBSTER THE LOBSTER (CAPTAIN CROOK'S FIENDISH BEAST OF A PET)

EXTRAS (TO FILL OUT THE SCENES AND MAKE IT LOOK ALL NICE AND BUSY)

"Auditions will be held on June 1st in this very place with a performance piece of your choice. Until then, dear hearts, farewell! May inspiration strike you strong! May good fortune meet you on this stage! And may the rotten-sea-cabbage-eating Stinker Shark never pass wind in your direction!"

I am definitely auditioning for the role of Jolly as a boy. This will be the perfect way to prove to Blackbeard and his horrible friends that I'm cool. I could be a famous pirate actor too! Star of stage and screen! My faithful sidekick, Boris, by my side as Carrot the Parrot!

We are going to be the most amazing double act EVER.

With a bit of luck, not many other pirates will give it a go.

12pm
Just chips for lunch . . .

APRIL 18TH

Every pirate on Crossbones Island wants to be in the movie!

We need a plan to increase our chances of success! Well, for a start, as Boris is a part-dragon, fire-breathing, gold-sniffing chicken, she doesn't exactly look much like a parrot.

I know — I've got a rainbow beret that Redruth SO kindly gave me one birthday when I mentioned I needed a new hat (after that unfortunate incident with the shark and the fishing rod). Boris could wear that. And I've borrowed some of

Mum's make-up – perfect for Boris's feathers.

All I need to do is persuade her she wants to wear feather make-up.

Hmm. That's "all".

I'm sure it'll be fine.

It shouldn't take long to make her look the part!

2pm

Oh, good grief. I am . . .

1. Repairing the window.

2. Bandaging Boris's wing.

3. Bandaging my big toe.

4. Pulling out forks that got stuck in the cabin wall.

5. Putting out the fire in my slippers.

6. Wiping make-up off the ceiling. And the walls. And the doors. And my hair . . .

7. Trying to persuade Boris to stop sulking with a large bowl of Chick-O-Snacks.

OK, so it could have gone better.

I'll knit her a nice woolly rainbow jumper instead . . .

MAY 9TH

Practising some lines. I once saw a play by this really clever playwright called William Sharkspear – Jolly was in it and I can remember some lines.

Just clearing my throat . . . Ahem!

"To sea, or not to sea: that is the question!"

Hmm. Is that the question? Not sure I've got that right. And, come to think of it, I don't know what the answer is either . . .

Or the next line . . .

But I'm going to practise that part anyway. Jolly will be so impressed that it's from a role he performed.

MAY 15TH

Blackbeard is auditioning for the role of Jolly too (drat)! He boarded my ship, quoted TWO SPEECHES from William Sharkspear, danced the hornpipe, slashed

BLACKBEARD IS A STAR

on the cabin door and took all my cupcakes.

Revenge shall be mine. MINE, I tell you!

Just as soon as I've repainted the cabin door, read and memorised *The Complete Works of William Sharkspear* and baked some more cupcakes.

MAY 31ST

It's the day before the audition.

Not nervous at all. Nope.

Just pure chance that I put my trousers on back to front and spread marmalade on my diary instead of on my toast.

Also just coincidence that Boris has been laying LOADS of green eggs all over the place. She's not nervous either. Nope. Not at all.

On the plus side: scrambled eggs for tea.

And breakfast . . .

And dinner . . .

And supper . . .

And a snack . . .

And more snacks . . .

We are going to be excellent. We are going to be FINE. I've finished knitting the jumper and persuaded Boris to put it on (by hiding Chick-O-Snacks in the sleeves).

Boris and I will prove how absolutely and completely marvellous we both are.

What could possibly go wrong?

Actually, better not think about that . . .

JUNE 1ST

Audition day!

Luckily, Boris's wing is out of the sling.

Unluckily, she's STILL in a bit of a
mood with me and wouldn't practise her
parrot-squawking.

At least she's wearing her parrot jumper,
and I know a couple of speeches off by
heart. I think.

9am

So I've had my ten scrambled eggs on

toast. (Should I be eating them if they're green . . .?) Tried to persuade Boris to get into the rowing boat to head to Crossbones Island. I promised her she could bring her favourite gold button with her.

In the end, I had to leave a trail of Chick-O-Snacks to get her out from under the bed, then swoop on her . . .

Well, a black eye, a fishing net and thirteen pecks later, we are finally in the boat. OK, I'm not looking my best now. And neither is Boris . . . But no time to stop and tidy ourselves up or we'll be late.

We <u>HAVE</u> to get to the audition or we'll miss out. This could change our fortunes forever! And I've come up with a brilliant stage name, much better than "Barnacles Blunderbeard"!

10am

At the Barrel Theatre. What a queue!
Everyone from Crossbones Island is here.

Standing behind me in the queue
is Captain Chomp, Senior Officer for
SMELLS (Society for Monsters Existing in
Large Lakes and Seas). He's got a HUGE
Giant DeathClaw Lobster in a HUGE
lobster pot on wheels. Wow, those creatures
are really rare!

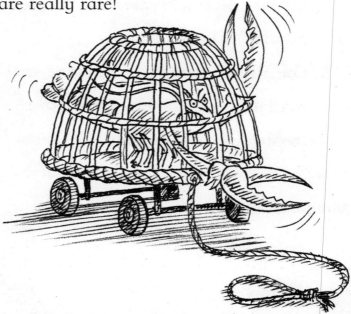

Captain Chomp must have brought him to audition for Mobster the Lobster. Yeek.

Wonder if Captain Chomp remembers it was me who:

1. Made his kraken sneeze constantly so that its tentacles got all tied up in plaits.
2. Accidentally ruined the digestive system of a rare giant piranha by feeding it baked beans.
3. Completely stressed out a load of giant man-eating eels and caused one to swallow a small plastic telescope.

Maybe he's forgotten . . .?

Captain Chomp's looking nervously at his lobster and glaring at me.

Don't think he's forgotten . . .

12.30pm

Loads of happy-looking pirates have had their auditions. Redruth and Blackbeard came out beaming.

The queue is getting shorter and shorter . . . We're inside the Barrel Theatre now.

Yeek! It's our turn! Taking a deep breath . . .

And on to the stage we go . . .

3.20pm

Well, that was interesting! Here's what happened.

Boris and I stood on the stage.

"Name?" Jolly boomed.

"Er . . . Tentacles Wonderbeard," I said. (Cool stage name, huh?) Boris's knees were knocking together.

Jolly looked at Boris and frowned doubtfully. "Is this a parrot I see before me?" he bellowed from the front row.

Oh dear. We were rumbled.

"Not entirely," I said, trying to sound like this was all planned. "It's a chicken in a cunning disguise."

I thought Jolly was going to go berserk. But he started laughing.

In fact, he laughed for eight minutes. Boris and I just looked at each other, wondering what we should do.

When Jolly stopped laughing at us, I cleared my throat. Ahem.

"To sea, or not to sea: that is the—"

SQUAWK! POP.

I couldn't believe it! Boris had laid a green egg on the stage! Right in the middle of my speech!

I cleared my throat again. Ahem.

"To sea, or not to—"

SQUAWK! POP.

"To sea—"

POP.

Oh. That. Chicken!!

Four minutes later, Jolly stopped laughing. AGAIN. My face was redder than Redruth's hair!

I had to do SOMETHING to show Jolly we were serious! That we were good!

Then I had one of my BRILLIANT ideas. I ran, opened the door and grabbed Captain Chomp and his giant lobster, and pulled them inside. This would show them that Boris COULD be Carrot the Parrot –

she's brave and brilliant enough to act alongside a ferocious beastie like Mobster the Lobster!

And <u>that</u> is when things REALLY started to go wrong . . .

I wonder if there's the teeniest, weeniest chance that Blackbeard won't hear about this. That's the problem with your rotten-faced, stinky-bummed big brother being director of PARPS (Pirates Against Rubbish Piracy Society). He takes any chance to come down on me like a ton of cannonballs. And I don't think Captain Chomp will exactly be putting in a good word for me. Grumph.

Expecting some letters in the mail tomorrow. ☹

JUNE 2ND

Yep.

Leviathan Cave
Secret Place
The Deep Dark Depths
The Ocean
June 1st

Dear Pirate Blunderbeard,

Congratulations – you have now upset the
ONLY Giant DeathClaw Lobster in the world!
I have spent the last EIGHT HOURS trying to
release its death-claw grip on my bottom!
   This is all your chicken's fault for laying a
green egg on the lobster's head, making it
panic and decide I was its mortal enemy for
bringing it to the theatre! Do you know how
hard it is to convince a Giant DeathClaw

Lobster that it wants to release the bottom of its mortal enemy? DO YOU?!

And when I finally got its claws open and freed my bottom, the lobster snapped its claws shut again, this time round my nose! DO YOU KNOW HOW HARD IT IS TO PERSUADE A RATHER CROSS LOBSTER TO LET GO OF ITS MORTAL ENEMY'S NOSE?! DO YOU?!

The poor creature is so stressed out, I have had to arrange yoga sessions to help it relax. DO YOU KNOW HOW HARD IT IS TO PERSUADE A VERY STRESSED-OUT GIANT DEATHCLAW LOBSTER TO TAKE UP YOGA?! DO YOU?!

I had a massive nosebleed over the stage – it took twenty handkerchiefs to stop it!

I therefore enclose a bill addressed to YOUR CHICKEN to pay for:

- a new mop for cleaning the stage
- twenty new handkerchiefs
- weekly yoga sessions for the lobster

If the lobster now doesn't get the part of Mobster the Lobster, I will personally hold YOU responsible.

Yours most furiously,

Captain Harry Chomp

Senior Officer,
Society for Monsters Existing in Large Lakes and Seas (SMELLS)
(Reg. charity 00000PS)

Huh! Captain Chomp thinks *the lobster* is stressed! He should see Boris! She wasn't very pleased that the lobster took her favourite gold button and started scuttling off with it. That's why she leapt at him and attacked him with a green egg!

Of course, she blames ME for everything.
Think that's why she set fire to my hat
after the audition when we were outside
the theatre. Fortunately, I managed to
throw it to one side before my eyebrows
got burned. Phew.

Pirates Against Rubbish Piracy Society

The Best Pirate Ship in the World

Dead Man's Cove

The Ocean

June 1st

Dear Barnacles Blunderbeard,

A GIANT DEATHCLAW LOBSTER ON
CAPTAIN CHOMP'S BOTTOM? ON. HIS.
BOTTOM?!! GREEN EGGS ALL OVER

THE STAGE? Are you out of your tiny, tiny mind?

PARPS is very excited that Jolly Roger has chosen to make his film on Crossbones Island and all of the PARPS pirates are looking forward to starring in the film. Therefore, if you cause trouble again, we shall be forced to take action. Of the very serious and rather cross type.

Yours hoping that you don't get a part in the film as I'm dreading your very existence on set,

Blasterous Blackbeard

(Director of PARPS)

P.S. And, if you haven't heard, I've got the part of the young Captain Crook!
I am going to be a star, so hah!

Grumph. Bet Blackbeard got that part easily. Dastardly, evil character? Just had to turn up and be himself. At least he doesn't get to play Jolly.

Oh well. I did the best I could. Audition success, on a scale of one to ten . . .? Well, I reckon I scraped a three. At least I didn't accidentally destroy the whole theatre or anything.

2pm

PIRATING TODAY
JUNE 2ND

GOLDEN EYEPATCH SURVIVES FIRE

Pirate Theatre Burnt Down: Flaming Hat Blamed

Whoops.

Pirates **A**gainst **R**ubbish **P**iracy **S**ociety

The Best Pirate Ship in the World

Dead Man's Cove

The Ocean

June 2nd

P.S. And if I ever find out that it was YOUR hat which burnt down the theatre, I will personally tie you to a mast and stuff a jellyfish down your trousers! Twice a day, for the rest of your life!

Blasterous Blackbeard

(Director of PARPS)

9.30am

Bought a new hat. Not much left of my old one. Ahem. It didn't look right without a shark bite taken out of it, so got Boris to peck a bit off the corner. That's better.

10.15am

Everyone's getting parts except for me. Redruth sent a message in her usual style, written on hot-pink paper wrapped round a cannonball. It knocked my *Pirating for Dummies* book off the shelf and into my plate of scrambled (green) eggs. She got the part of Jolly's sister, Polly Roger.

Hmm . . . Just beginning to wonder if they might not want us . . .

Baked cupcakes to stop me feeling nervous.

Forgot to put oven on. Think I'm still nervous.

11am

Yeek! Jolly's famous, award-winning
parrot, Romeo, is heading for my ship!
(Just as well he's retired otherwise *he*
would have taken the role of Carrot!) He's
clutching a letter! Oh no. Now what?
Maybe it's telling me I've got to pay to
rebuild the Barrel Theatre. Or that I'm not
allowed anywhere near filming, or—

ARGH! Romeo just dropped the
letter on my face. Opening it now!

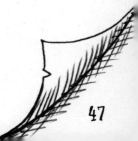

The Glittering Starfish

Dead Man's Cove

June 16TH

Dear Tentacles Wonderbeard,

What a marvellous comedy performance! Such magnificent timing! What man could set his eyes upon that stage and fail to notice your great potential?

It is therefore with the greatest of pleasure that I offer you the role of Jolly Roger in PLOP: The Movie! (Regrettably the part of Carrot the Parrot has been assigned to a real parrot as your chicken still looked like a chicken in a jumper and a rainbow beret.)

I look forward to seeing you on the first day of filming: August 20th. Your script will follow presently for you to learn. Until then, may good fortune speed your footsteps! May the west wind fill your sails! And may the extra-sharp-and-pointy Spiky Sea Urchin never meet your bottom.

Yours sincerely,

Jolly Roger

ABSOLUTELY BRILLIANT ACTOR/
DIRECTOR/ALL-ROUND STAR
GOLDEN EYEPATCH WINNER –
BEST ACTOR

Comedy act? But I was doing serious acting . . . NEVER MIND! I can't believe it! I've got a part! And not just any part – THE BEST PART!

Doing a celebration dance with Boris.

(Wonder if we can get that in the film?)

Going to bake the most enormous chocolate fudge cupcake to celebrate! And filming starts August 20th! My birthday!

I'M GOING TO BE A STAR!

11.05am

A STAR!!!!!!!!!

JULY 4TH

9am

Still can't believe I've got the part! I
wonder who is going to play Carrot
the Parrot, my faithful sidekick? Such a
shame it's not Boris. She's still wearing the
rainbow beret. Seems rather fond of it now.

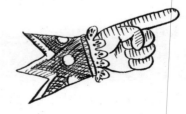

Pirates **A**gainst **R**ubbish **P**iracy **S**ociety

The Best Pirate Ship in the World

Dead Man's Cove

The Ocean

July 3RD

Dear Blunderbeard,

It is with great delight and pride that PARPS is writing to inform you that a wonderfully talented bird has landed the part of Carrot the Parrot in *PLOP: The Movie* – IronClaw!

IronClaw is very much looking forward to appearing in the movie and we are especially chuffed that a PARPS parrot has been chosen, especially as he is mine. Therefore, any stupidity on your part will be dealt with harshly. To summarise:

DON'T YOU DARE MUCK THIS UP.

Yours really very sincerely,

Blasterous Blackbeard

(Director of PARPS)

P.S. And do not forget that I trained him to poo on your toothbrush. (That was a great summer.)

P.P.S. Oh yeah, congratulations on getting the part. Make the most of it before Jolly realises the mistake he's made and changes his mind.

IRONCLAW?!

Blackbeard's parrot hates me almost as much as Blackbeard does! But I will not let this spoil my big moment. Jolly thinks I'm amazing and I'm going to be the star of *PLOP: The Movie!*

. . . G
    u
     l
      p.

With the evil Parrot of Darkness on my shoulder. Better not mention the word "plop" to him . . .

JULY 19TH

9am

OH. THAT. CHICKEN! A bottle floated
by outside my ship with the script inside,
addressed to "Tentacles Wonderbeard". Boris
came marching over, so I showed it to her
and told her not to worry she didn't get the
part: she can still come and watch me filming
with the parrot. And what did she do?

She snatched the script in her beak.

Threw it on the floor. Jumped up and down on it. Tore it to shreds with her feet. Put the shreds in my cannon. Fired them out to sea. Gave an enormous fart in my direction and stomped off.

Chickens! I will never understand them!

Better ask for a new script.

I think it's just possible Boris may have a

teeny-weeny bit of a jealousy problem . . .

Learning script.

Still learning script.

Long script . . .

AUGUST 20TH

9am

Happy birthday to me! Filming starts today! That's the best birthday present! I'm so excited. Mum sent a birthday card saying good luck. Boris is still huffy and refused to light my birthday candles with her flames. I've said she can come along on set AS LONG AS SHE DOESN'T CAUSE TROUBLE. (I really don't want parrot-poo on my toothbrush again.) I'm sure she'll be fine.

I have to go to Barber Rossa for hair and make-up first. I'll look great.

10am

Been to hair and make-up. I look . . . um . . .
great.

10.30am

Jolly is late – he's doing an interview with *Pirate Monthly* and apparently can't stop talking, so he sent a message telling us to start without him.

Blackbeard is coming over with IronClaw. Ha! Looks like IronClaw has been to hair and make-up too!

Caught Boris glaring at me and then at IronClaw. She looks as pleased as a shark whose false teeth have fallen out.

Hmm, don't suppose Blackbeard has come over to wish me a happy birthday. What's he up to? Blackbeard is whispering something to the Evil Parrot of Darkness. IronClaw has hopped onto my shoulder . . .

ARGH! Here comes the cameraman, ready for my opening shot – when I'm faced with the dreaded Mobster the Lobster. He's waiting over there, with Captain Chomp. Good job that Boris hasn't seen him. They didn't exactly get on brilliantly at the Barrel Theatre . . .

URGH! IronClaw has pooed down my neck! Oh. That. Evil Parrot of Darkness! Can't believe I'm going to say my opening lines as a film star with parrot poo going right down my—

Cameraman's ready! In THREE,

TWO,

ONE—

ARGH!

OH. THAT. CHICKEN!

The camera started rolling and Boris leapt for my shoulder — she's knocked IronClaw flying with a karate move!

IronClaw's landed right on the camera. Oh no! The cameraman has dropped the camera! He's staggering backwards . . . Look out for the—! Oops. Man holding the light. Now *he's* falling over! Watch out for the—! Oh dear. Lady holding the microphone. Mind out for— Oops. Boris. Who has just burped loudly into the microphone. Oh. Good. Grief.

And now the lobster is scuttling off with the microphone. Why on the Seven Seas would it want a microphone?

The sound-woman snatches it back and gets a nip on the nose for her trouble.

Everyone is furious. Including me. I've told Boris no more Chick-O-Snacks for the rest of the week. That'll teach her to—ARGH! She's set fire to my fake eyebrows!

Need to stick my head in a barrel of water!

Phew. That's better.

Oh dear. Filming cancelled for the rest of the day while they replace everything.

2pm
Letter arrived. Suppose I have to open it?

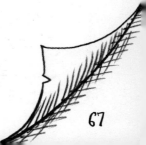

Pirates **A**gainst **R**ubbish **P**iracy **S**ociety

The Best Pirate Ship in the World

Dead Man's Cove

The Ocean

August 20th

Blunderbeard,

We are warning you: keep that feather-brained creature under control! One more stupid stunt and we will have no choice but to REMOVE YOUR CHICKEN until all filming has finished.

As punishment for terrorising an innocent parrot, you must send over a large packet of prawn crackers for IronClaw and a dozen peanut-butter cupcakes for me this afternoon.

Yours exceedingly furiously,

Blasterous Blackbeard

(Director of PARPS)
P.S. Happy birthday.

I don't want to be de-chickened! Boris may be a pain sometimes, but she's the only friend I have. Have explained to Boris that if she annoys IronClaw again, she's eating sea-cabbage stew for the rest of the month – and I'll take back the rainbow beret.

AUGUST 21ST

9am

Jolly is doing part two of the *Pirate Monthly* interview (apparently the interviewer begged to go to bed and asked if they could finish off in the morning), so Jolly said to carry on with the assistant director as we're on a tight schedule. (Hmm, even tighter than Jolly knows after yesterday's Craziest Chicken of the Year incident!)

Cameraman's here with a new camera (looking upset). IronClaw is on my shoulder (looking smug). Boris is glaring from the side (looking jealous). Ah, there's Captain Chomp (looking nervous) with the Giant DeathClaw Lobster (looking vicious), ready to be set on me for the opening fight scene! It's snapping its claws, ready to attack . . . GULP. I hope Captain Chomp can control that thing . . .

And we're on in THREE,

TWO,

ONE—

ARGH!

OH. THAT. CHICKEN!

What's she doing now?! She's flapping in front of me – she's attacking the lobster! Boris, I'm fine, you crazy bird! We're just acting! Neptune's knickers!

There's an epic battle going on: lobster vs chicken! The rainbow beret goes flying.

Good grief, I think chicken is winning!
She's obviously doing really well in
her karate lessons! Defeated, the Giant
DeathClaw Lobster scuttles off at the rate
of knots. Boris looking very pleased. Um,
Captain Chomp not so much . . . He's
stormed off to get his lobster back.

12pm

Oh dear. Filming cancelled for the day while they find the lobster. Just as well. Boris and me need to find her rainbow beret. It got lost in the fight. Boris is not pleased.

1pm

Oh dear. No sign of beret. Boris in a really bad mood with me.

5pm

The lobster must have been found in the end. Just been to pick up fish and chips for lunch and seen an upset-looking Captain Chomp and his DeathClaw pet boarding

Jolly's ship. Probably going to complain about me and Boris . . .

At least I get to eat the haddock today.

5.15pm

Letter waiting for me. Sigh.

Pirates Against Rubbish Piracy Society

The Best Pirate Ship in the World

Dead Man's Cove

The Ocean

August 21st

Blunderbeard,

Karate-chopping the leading lobster?

This time your chicken has gone too far.
As soon as their filming schedules allow,
representatives from PARPS will arrive and
officially de-chicken you. She will be kept

at Pirate Pete's pet shop. You can have your ridiculous pet back when filming is finished and not a moment before. Do not, **REPEAT, DO NOT** bring your chicken to work tomorrow.

And watch your step. Any more trouble and you'll be banned as well. (Then maybe someone more deserving will get your part. Like me.)

Yours so crossly
that I just
accidentally
jumped up and down
on my hat and threw it in the sea, which
is also completely your fault,

Blasterous Blackbeard

(Director of PARPS)

OH NO! BORIS! What have you done? ☹

In my shock, accidentally dropped the haddock overboard.

Just chips for lunch again . . .

AUGUST 22ND

Have left Boris at home. She's not impressed. I can't believe they are going to take her away.

Jolly's finished his interview so he should be here. But why is he late? Assistant director said to make a start. Cameraman's ready.

And we're on in THREE – at last, my chance to shine!

TWO – I'll be famous!

ONE – I'll show YOU, Blackbeard!

And—

There's Jolly! He's running towards us! His hands are flapping around! He looks like he's panicking . . .

Oh. Good. Grief. He's saying this:

"My trophy! My trophy! All my treasure for my trophy!"

What?

"Stop the filming! A curse be upon us for some cruel, heartless thief has stolen my beloved Golden Eyepatch trophy! Everywhere have I searched but no trace can be found!"

WHAT?

"Filming cannot and will not continue until my trophy has been returned! A reward greater than a thousand galleons for the brave-hearted soul who finds it:

whatever role they choose in the movie. And a fate worse than a thousand deaths for the villain who stole it! May your eyes be sharp! May your feet be quick! And may the lesser spotted Toe-Stubber Crab never cross your path!"

WHAT?!

I don't believe it! Finally I have a chance — the biggest chance I'll ever have to be someone special — and Jolly's refusing to let filming continue! I must find that Golden Eyepatch. No way I'm letting Blackbeard — or any other pirate — find it first! Everyone will want to play Jolly and I *must* have this chance in the film. Thank

Neptune I've got something no other pirate has: a gold-sniffing, part-dragon chicken at home! That'll speed things up.

Oh no. Here comes Blackbeard. And he's smiling. I hate it when he looks happy. It means I'm about to be miserable.

WHAT?!!

He said that as filming is cancelled, they're coming to get Boris now!

Today really couldn't get any worse—

Argh! Flopped down on the ground in despair. Sat on extra-sharp-and-pointy Spiky Sea Urchin.

Life stinks.

2pm

Back on my boat. Boris doesn't understand she's being taken away ☹. I feel bad about being cross with her on set. She was only trying to help. Sort of . . . I think she's trying to say sorry for being huffy as she sniffed out a gold coin I'd dropped down the back of the sofa ages ago and gave it to me. I'll keep that in my pocket. You never know when that'll come in handy!

Oh, I can't let Blackbeard take my chicken! She's my only friend, and I won't stand a chance of finding the Golden Eyepatch without her. There must be something I can do?

Ideas:

1. Hide somewhere on ship

2. Escape and hope we can outrun
   all the brilliantly fast ships which
   belong to PARPS (only if my ship
   sprouted wings and flew)

3. Let PARPS take Boris

NEVER!!!!!

☹

2.35pm

Shhh. Hiding in a barrel with Boris.

Wonder how many pirates have hidden in a barrel with a gold-sniffing chicken before. PARPS will be here any moment. They. Must. Not. Find. Us.

2.41pm
Voices! PARPS are coming!

Right, Boris — no farting, no sneezing, no squawking, no clucking, no flapping. Got it?

2.42pm
OH. THAT. CHICKEN!!!!!!

She didn't fart, she didn't sneeze, she didn't squawk, she didn't cluck, she didn't flap . . .

SHE BELCHED!

She thinks doing flame-burps is a fun way to pass the time – while we are HIDING IN A BARREL, TRYING NOT TO BE DETECTED!

Argh! Barrel filling with smoke. Coughing lots! Will just lift the lid off a bit to get some fresh air.

Ah. That'll be the sound of my smoke alarm going off, then.

FOOTSTEPS!

VOICES!

BLACKBEARD!

ARGHHHHHHHH!

2.58pm

Off she goes on the PARPS ship. Bye-bye,
Boris. Rotten Blackbeard. Revenge shall
definitely be mine this time. Somehow.

Somewhen. Or my name isn't Barnacles
Bernard Biggleswade Blunderbeard.
Which, unfortunately, it is.

AUGUST 23RD

Have packed Boris a little suitcase and
posted it to Pirate Pete's Pets. I included
her favourite things – some packets of
Chick-O-Snacks and her gold button to
cuddle at night. I wish we'd found her
rainbow beret. I could have sent that too.
Wonder what happened to it . . .

It's not the same without Boris.

I'll write her a poem.

Oh, Boris, you chicken of such little brain,

Oh, how I do wish I could see you again.

Your scruffy old feathers, your scrawny old legs.

'Cos now you have gone, I have run out of eggs.

Hmm. Maybe not.

I shall try to get over this most tragic loss by being extra busy in my quest to find the Golden Eyepatch. But how to find the patch without Boris?

AUGUST 28TH

Blunderbeard's WonderWeird Contraptions
are proud to Introduce the **Stuffhunter™**.

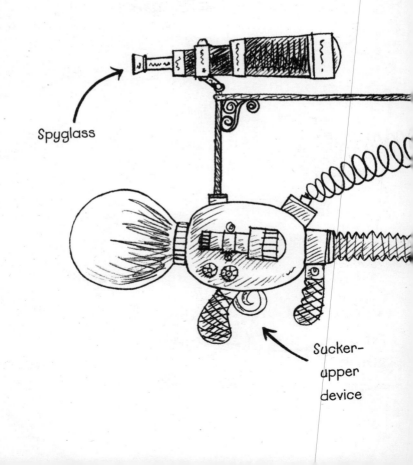

Spyglass

Sucker-
upper
device

What if Jolly has just dropped the trophy on his ship? No one else is looking there and this invention will help me do it quickly!

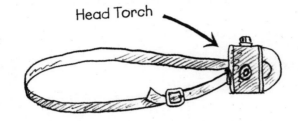

Head Torch

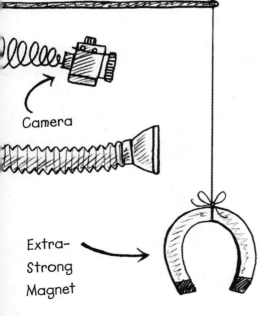

Camera

Extra-Strong Magnet

With a bit of luck, I'll find the patch dropped down the back of an old treasure chest or something on Jolly's boat, save the day, get my reward and get back to filming! Maybe I'll even be allowed to have Boris back.

A perfect plan!

3pm

...With one or two drawbacks, as it turns out.

OK, maybe I should have tested the StuffHunter™ first.

But how was I supposed to know the magnet was going to be strong enough to make Jolly's belt burst its belt loops and come hurtling towards it, making Jolly's trousers fall down?

And how was I supposed to know he was wearing pink polka-dot underpants . . . or that the camera on the concertina would spring into action and take a photo of him RIGHT at that moment?

Or that the sucker-upper (which was meant to clear away the dust and dirt behind treasure chests so I could search better) was going to accidentally suck off Jolly's beard and moustache? (I didn't even know they were fake!)

Or that the bright torch would dazzle him so he couldn't see where he was going . . . OR see the lesser spotted Toe-Stubber Crab, which JUST HAPPENED to cross the deck as he stumbled forwards . . .

As I say . . . HOW WAS I SUPPOSED TO KNOW?!

Jolly doesn't look very jolly at the moment. Whoops.

Pirates **A**gainst **R**ubbish **P**iracy **S**ociety

The Best Pirate Ship in the World

Dead Man's Cove

The Ocean

August 28th

BLUNDERBEARD!!!!!!!

😐 😐 😐 😐 😐 😐 😐 😐 😐 😐

His toes? His BEARD? HIS PANTS?! Do you have to upset, ruin or explode everything you meet!? Be aware that now Jolly has finished his *Pirate Monthly* interview, he's had a chance to read my reports on exactly why filming was delayed: HOW his camera and lights got broken and WHY his starring lobster did a runner for the afternoon!

Needless to say, Jolly is NOT in a good mood at the moment. Say goodbye to

your role in the movie, Blunderbeard,

and to any chance of finding the Golden

Eyepatch. We are coming around

tomorrow to inform you of your very

big and nasty punishment for all

the very big and nasty trouble

you have caused.

Yours more sincerely than ever,

Blasterous Blackbeard

Director of PARPS

Yep. That pretty much sums it up. ☹

Imagine a **big pile** of trouble. Nope, **bigger** than that. Right. Now, place it on top of

ANOTHER

big pile

of

trouble.

My head is sticking out of the top of the pile. With rotten tomatoes being thrown at it.

AUGUST 29TH

9am

☹ ☹ ☹ ☹ ☹ ☹ ☹ ☹ ☹

What am I going to do?

Blackbeard and Jolly came around in person. They were furious. Jolly was actually hopping from foot to foot, really "hopping mad". Although maybe that was still because of the lesser spotted Toe-Stubber Crab. He even said that he hoped the rotten-sea-cabbage-eating Stinker-Shark DID pass wind in my direction. ☹

And worse than that: a new Pirate Law has just been passed! This is what it says:

It is hereby declared that from this day forward, one PIRATE BARNACLES BERNARD BIGGLESWADE BLUNDERBEARD, also known, rather stupidly, as TENTACLES WONDERBEARD, is completely and utterly and TOTALLY banned from the entirety of Crossbones Island until the Golden Eyepatch trophy has been found.

As punishment for his ridiculous acts of disgrace, he will immediately be:

1) Forced to wear the frilly Bloomers of Shame on the outside of his trousers.

2) Forced to wear the pink flowery

Bonnet of Ridicule, and watch his pirate hat being ripped to shreds by a Giant DeathClaw Lobster.

3) Paraded through Crossbones Island with everyone laughing at him. A lot.

4) Shipped out to the Rather Big Rock Where We Put Naughty People We are Really Fed Up With — taking no clean underpants, no picnic, NOTHING.

Signed,

Captain Skwidd

Captain Skwidd

Pirate Overlord and

Toughest Pirate on the Seas

They are coming back tomorrow when
I shall face my doom.

My reputation as pirate is officially
RUINED. FOREVER.

11am
Been forced to wear the Bonnet of
Ridicule and the Bloomers of Shame.
Redruth was kind enough to take a photo.
Grrr. She said it might come in useful if
there are any "Stupidest Pirate of the Year"
competitions. Although, she also said I'd
probably win without entering anyway.
Double GRRR.

Think the bonnet would suit Boris

... Perhaps it'll make up for the lost

rainbow beret. Wonder if I get to keep it?

12pm

They gave my hat to the Giant DeathClaw Lobster. I thought it would enjoy tearing my hat to pieces, but it just grabbed it and scuttled off. Humph. Probably the last I'll see of that.

Walked through the streets. Everyone laughed. I lifted up my head like I didn't care ... and the Bonnet of Ridicule slipped over my eyes. Tripped over my feet. Went head over heels (well, bonnet over bloomers)

and ended up at Blackbeard's feet. He said I deserved this, and good riddance.

1pm

Blackbeard is personally rowing me out to the Rather Big Rock Where We Put Naughty People We are Really Fed Up With. No pirate has been sent here for years. Think last time was when Captain Cutthroat sank all the pirate ships in Harbour Grudge for a bet, and then ate all the cheese on the island. No pizza for anyone that night. They were REALLY upset.

And now it's my turn. I only wanted to be in the movie.

I really am the Worst. Pirate. Ever.☹

2pm

At the Rock. No clean pants, no picnic.

No ice-cream boats floating about selling

ice creams. Nothing.

Just have to sit here and wait. They said

if I'm good they might send a parrot to

drop some food for me.

I wish Boris was here. Going to pass the

time carving a chicken picture into the Rock.

2.30pm
Carving not
going very well.

Blackbeard's parrot IronClaw dropped a food parcel:

- One half-eaten cheese sandwich

- One opened packet of crisps (with five crisps left)

- Three pieces of seaweed. (I hate raw seaweed.)

- A mouldy orange

10.49am

Seagull stole the sandwich. Grumph.

Wonder what Boris is doing.

2pm

I am doomed to stay here forever. I must

have been here at least five years!

   Have given up carving chicken on Rock.

   Going for something easier.

Carving picture of cupcake on Rock.

2.45pm

Given up carving cupcake.

   Carving picture of "straight line" on

Rock.

Right. I need to stop feeling sorry for myself and find that trophy!

All I need to do is:

1) **Un-maroon myself from the Rather Big Rock which happens to be in The Middle of the Ocean,**

2) **Rescue my gold-sniffing chicken from Pirate Pete's Pets,**

3) **Track down the Golden Eyepatch and**

4) **Save the day.**

Aha! A plan!

Right . . . Number one, then . . . Un-maroon myself!

Umm ...

Hmm ...

Bit stuck.

Parrot drop!

- One banana (squished)
- Four carrot sticks (nibbled)
- Bottle of lemonade (not bubbly)
- And a letter from Blackbeard ...

Pirates Against Rubbish Piracy Society

The Best Pirate Ship in the World

Dead Man's Cove

The Ocean

September 2ND

Dear Blunderbeard,

We are writing to inform you that your chicken has the appetite of a whale and the manners of a sea cucumber. She has caused utter chaos at Pirate Pete's Pets since arriving. We therefore have no choice but to deduct £50 from your treasure chest at YoHo Bank to pay for:

- More Chick-O-Snacks (she's eaten all of Pirate Pete's supply).
- A bottle of ChickaPoo For Today's Constipated Chicken (*because* she's eaten all of Pirate Pete's Chick-O-Snack supply).
- A new hat for the Director of PARPS as she burnt the last one (because she was upset that there were no more Chick-O-Snacks after she'd eaten all of Pirate Pete's supply).

When you get off the Rock, PARPS strongly suggest you enrol your chicken in behaviour

management classes. And put her on
a diet.

Yours crossly and despairing at the pair
of you,

Blasterous Blackbeard

Director of PARPS

P.S. Try not to break the Rock while
you're there. And whatever you do, don't
carve anything on it. Captain Skwidd
goes crazy if anyone does that.
P.P.S. Mum says hi.

Hahaha! Good old Boris. I hope she's taking her ChickaPoo medicine nicely. It's yucky stuff. I remember that once – due to events which were *entirely* not my fault – I ended up having to drink it myself and then used the poo-medicine bottle to send a message to PARPS! Even THAT wasn't as embarrassing as the Bonnet of Ridicule and the Bloomers of Shame.

Oh, if ONLY I could get off this rock. I know I'd be breaking every pirate rule, but maybe, with Boris's superb sniffability, we could get the Golden Eyepatch trophy back!

But HOW can I get off this rock?

Wait a minute! That's it! A message

in a bottle! Not a ChickaPoo bottle this time but my lemonade bottle. And I can write on the inside of my cheese-sandwich wrapper. (No bins here – you have to take your rubbish home with you.) Someone's bound to find it. And I've still got that gold coin in my pocket that Boris sniffed out from the back of the sofa! That could pay for someone to take me back to the island!

Ladies and gentlemen, we have a plan. Blunderbeard is back in business!

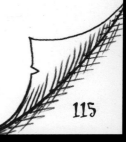

To Whomever Finds This Letter,

Er, hello! I'm in a little bit of a pickle,

stranded on the Rather Big Rock Where

We Put Naughty People We are Really

Fed Up With. I need to get off right

away, as I think I can find Jolly Roger's

Golden Eyepatch with the help of my

gold-sniffing chicken.

　　If you come and get me, there will

be a gold coin waiting for you (a really nice shiny one) and I promise not to tell anyone it was you who rescued me, and I'll also bake you loads of cupcakes to say thank you.

Please come soon.

From

Barnacles Blunderbeard

P.S. And please bring a bag of chips with you. The food here is awful.

My bottle has been sent.

I'm ready to go.

3pm

No boats.

7pm

No boats.

Or chips.

SEPTEMBER 5TH

10.19am

Just wondering if there's a teensy chance
my plan won't work?

Surely it will, though. Pirates are so

naughty, surely someone will break a rule in exchange for a bit of treasure and some cupcakes?

Writing a victory song to pass the time:

All alone upon a rock, in the freezing cold,

No clean pants, no picnic. The only things I hold:

A squished banana, nibbled cheese, an orange full of mould,

But I am going to save the day and find the Patch of Gold.

And now my story will become a legend ever told,

Of how I left the dreadful rock to find my chicken bold,

I'll be a pirate hero, even though I'm not that old,

For I am going to save the day and find the Patch of Gold.

Yes, we are going to save the day and find the Patch of Gold!

11.04am

No boats.

1.16pm

BOAT!!!!!!!!!!!

Captain Orlando Hoy from Lando Hoy ferries found my bottle and picked me up!

He was really pleased with the treasure.
Says he's not seen a gold coin like that for
years. (Yes, well, that's because it's been lost
down the sofa for ages.)

Tried to sing my victory song but
Captain Hoy said to stop that awful noise
or he'd take me back to the rock. Had to
hum quietly instead.

3pm

Landed at Crossbones Island. I needed to sneak across the island to Pirate Pete's Pets without looking suspicious – or like me! So I crept from coconut tree to coconut tree until I arrived at Barber Rossa's. No one was there. Everyone must have been looking for the Golden Eyepatch.

Have put my Bloomers of Shame *under* my trousers, tucked the bonnet inside my waistcoat and borrowed a wig from Barber Rossa's cupboard. (He keeps some in case a haircut goes really, reeeeally bad.) I'm sure he won't mind. There was only one left – the rest are being used for the movie. I'll put it back afterwards. There

were also some fake beards. They must
be spare ones for Jolly, you know, in case
someone accidentally sucks them off with
an invention or something. Ahem.

Have taken a beard for Boris — she'll
have to be disguised too.

Really don't like this wig. Long ... red ...
I look like cousin Redruth. As long as she
never, ever sees me looking like—

4.05pm

I don't believe it! The whole of Crossbones
Island, and I had to bump into my cousin.

Yes, she laughed.

Yes, she took a photo ☹.

Still, could be worse. Could have been

Blackbeard who found me. Or Jolly! She's
promised not to blab to Blackbeard that
I'm here. That's good of her. Maybe I
won't try to get rid of her after all . . .

Now. Time to get me a chicken!

5pm

Hiding behind a barrel of parrot feed at Pirate Pete's Pets. I spot a chicken!

Coast looks clear.

I'm coming, Boris!

5.02pm

I reeeeeeeeally don't believe it!

She's completely ignoring me. Why isn't she pleased to see me?!

5.04pm

Aha! Another Brilliant Blunders plan. I reached through the cage bars and took her favourite gold button.

Now she's paying attention. ☺

Ah . . . She's a bit upset about the whole button thing actually. ☹

Er . . . Pecking a lot at the bars now. Flapping crossly . . . Squawking . . . Oh, my ears!

Oooh . . . She's dented the cage door. Great, I can get the door open now. There!

Ah . . . Slight problem. Now she's loose . . . And pecking ME! ARGH! Boris, stop! It's ME!

5.06pm

Ohhhhhhhhhhh, I know what's wrong.

Taking off the red wig . . . Phew! Now she's realised who I am.

Have given her back her gold button. Ah, she IS pleased to see me (now she has her treasure back, tucked under her feathers).

No time to lose! I've put my wig back on. Boris is wearing her beard. Hmm . . . kind of suits her.

Right! Have explained to Boris we're on a mission! We're going to save the day and find the Patch of Gold! (Cue the song!)

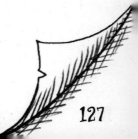

5.09pm

Yeek! We're outside Pirate Pete's shop.

Pirates are dashing everywhere, trying
to be first to find the Golden Eyepatch.
Others are accusing each other and sword-
fighting in the streets (though maybe that's
just because it's fun).

But we will find it first! Because I have
a part-dragon chicken who can sniff gold
a mile away. Haha! Ready, Boris, and
. . . go!

And . . . GO!

AND . . . GO!!!!

Or . . . not.

She's sniffing around but hasn't got the scent of it at all! Why not? How far away could it be?!

Go, Boris, GO!

No, not to the toilet! Oh. That. Chicken! How much ChickaPoo did they give you?! Pirate Pete won't be pleased about that all over his floor.

This is a disaster! Boris can't sniff the trophy out, so we can't find it that way, and I can't use any of my inventions because that will blow my disguise completely, so we can't find it *that* way!

Oh dear.

Oh. Very. VERY. Dear.

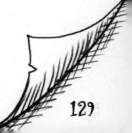

There's just one thing for it: Boris and I are going to have to use our brains.

H e l p.

5.15pm

No problem. I'll think of a plan.

5.45pm

I will.

6.45pm

Maybe . . .

7pm

A loud bell is ringing out! The pirates have put their swords away and stopped fighting. And they're not dashing around looking for the trophy. What's going on? They're all heading to the remains of the Barrel Theatre – except Captain Chomp. Hmm. He's walking the other way with that pesky DeathClaw Lobster in its lobster pot on wheels. Probably going home to put it to bed with a hot-water bottle and a teddy bear.

Tiptoeing behind the pirates to find out what's going on.

Ah.

Seen a poster up.

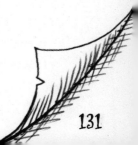

SEPTEMBER 5ᵀᴴ 7PM–9PM
BARREL THEATRE
(REMAINS OF)

PIRATE MONTHLY WILL BE FILMING A

SPECIAL TELEVISION DOCUMENTARY LIVE:

THE TRAGEDY OF THE LOST GOLDEN EYEPATCH AWARD

ALL PIRATES WELCOME TO TAKE PART

PIRATE PETS NOT WELCOME
(DUE TO RECENT EVENTS – *TROUBLE FROM A CERTAIN CHICKEN* – WE DO NOT WANT TO RISK ANIMALS DISTURBING THE RECORDING.)

Ah, these pirates will be there for a while. Maybe this is my chance to get ahead.

If only I had any kind of idea where to start looking. But I don't. All I have is a bearded chicken and—

WAIT A MINUTE!
CAPTAIN CHOMP!

Of course! He was with Jolly the evening before the Golden Eyepatch went missing! I saw him when I went to get my fish and chips. Then, the next morning, the Golden Eyepatch was gone! Hmm. Maybe Captain Chomp knows something about all this. I need to find out! I'll go and do some investigating tonight!

I'm a bit scared. There are some really

weird, dangerous creatures at his home . . .

He lives at Leviathan Cave, Secret Place (so all his angry letters to me say). No idea where that is (guess that's why it's called Secret Place) but I can still just about see Captain Chomp disappearing. We'll follow him and hope he doesn't see us! But, if he does, hopefully he'll think I'm still on the Rock and won't suspect a pirate with long red hair and a bearded bird.

Right, Boris – SHHHHHHHHH HHHHHH!

7.10pm

We followed Captain Chomp to the harbour. He and the lobster set off in a rowing boat, and we headed after them in Blackbeard's. Sure he won't mind if we just borrow it for a little bit . . .

It's so windy out here on the ocean that I've had to put on the Bonnet of Ridicule to stop my wig from blowing away. How many other pirates in the world EVER have rowed a boat at night wearing a ridiculous bonnet with a bearded chicken for company?! Probably fewer than one—

HEY! Boris! Get off! That's MY Bonnet of Ridicule! You've got your beard!

Grumph.

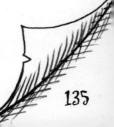

7.30pm

Right, we're rounding a corner of Crossbones Island now. Never been up this far before.

I can just about see Captain Chomp ahead . . . Is he wearing a clothes peg on his nose? Why would he do that? He's disappearing into a cave that opens onto the sea. The waves are dragging us towards it. Oooh, it looks really dark in there. ☹

NUMBER 2, SECRET PLACE, SMELLS HEADQUARTERS

NO ENTRY. TRESPASSERS WILL BE GOBBLED UP BY A VARIETY OF CREATURES BEFORE YOU CAN SAY "FANG-TOOTHED GLOWFISH".

DELIVERIES ROUND THE BACK, PLEASE.

Yeek! That doesn't sound good. But what choice do we have? We need to find that Golden Eyepatch. So we need to follow Captain Chomp.

Boris – we're going in!

7.32pm

Have lost sight of Captain Chomp. It's so dark in here.

Wish I could see where we are going . . .

Ah, that's better. There's a bit of light coming from somewhere and—

BORIS! Why are you— what are you— that's MY BONNET OF RIDICULE you're wearing! Give it back! Oh. That. Chicken. Better just let her keep it. (Does suit her. Thought it would. Guess that makes up for the rainbow beret.)

Light's getting very bright now.

Coming from right beside the boat . . .

Almost as if it's floating alongside us . . .

Like a great . . . big . . . giant . . .

ARGH! FANG-TOOTHED GLOWFISH! It's taken a bite out of the boat! Its teeth are like daggers! Its eyes are like torches!

It's coming for another bite!

Boris has jumped on my lap – can't see anything past her stupid Bonnet of Ridicule.

CRUNCH! ARGH!

There's a path over there along the cave wall. We're going to have to jump for it, right over the Fang-Toothed Glowfish. It's that or be gobbled up ... Good luck, Boris!
ONE – TWO – THREE ...!

7.35pm

We made it in one piece. Which is more than can be said for Blackbeard's boat. Yeek. Will have a bit of explaining to do there.

Never mind, we're alive (until Blackbeard finds out about his boat anyway).

Tiptoeing along the cave path.

What is that AWFUL, AWFUL stench!? No wonder this place is the SMELLS headquarters! Boris has wrapped the beard round her beak to block it out. Will have to hold my nose.

Walking along the path. At least there are no more creatures to—

OW!!!!!!!!!!!!!!!!!

My toe! Boris
squawks and
hops into my
arms – argh!
There are loads
of lesser spotted
Toe-Stubber
Crabs scuttling
right towards us! No
wonder they are lesser
spotted. All the Toe-Stubber Crabs in the
world seem to be guarding this place!

There's a tunnel veering off to the right.
Quick, Boris – let's

hop

for it!

7.40pm

Phew.

Bet Captain Chomp doesn't have many visitors. Or at least many visitors LEFT by the end of their visit!

Yuck. The smell! It's like rotten sea cabbage mixed with Blackbeard's socks!

Boris is scared and wants to be carried. Giving her a piggyback, though, otherwise I can't see over her bonnet. How many pirates in the history of EVER have worn a long red wig and carried a bearded chicken in a ridiculous bonnet on their backs WHILST hopping down a tunnel? If PARPS saw me now I'd be back on the Rock for the rest of my life!

At the end of the tunnel. There's a big room with another tunnel leading off at the end. And the room is full of—

W O W !

So many weird and wonderful creatures! There's a baby Loch Ness Monster, and a three-finned Sting-Nose Fish and, oh! A kraken – with its tentacles in plaits, snot dripping from its nose . . . It's the one I fought with at the Pirate of the Year competition, when I single-handedly discovered krakens had a pepper allergy. Wonder if it remembers me . . .

ARGH!

THE **ELASTICATED** BEARD! SHE'S JUST PINGED DOWN THE ROOM. AM LEFT CLUTCHING BEARD. NOW SHE'S HOPPING FOR IT!

BORIS, **COME BACK!**

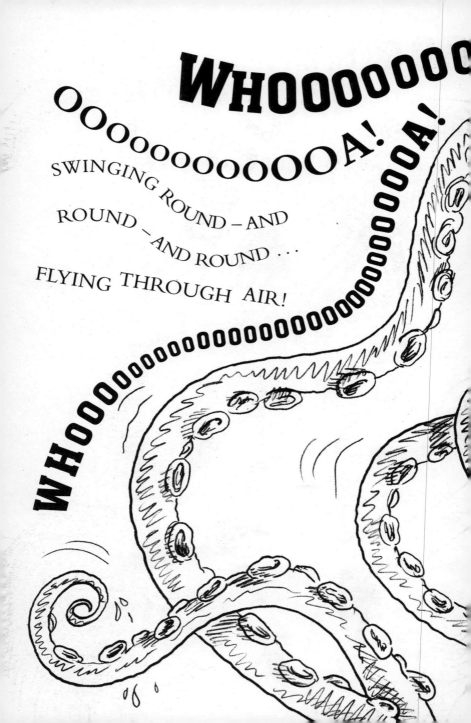

WHOOOOOOO
OOOOOOOOOOOOA!
SWINGING ROUND – AND
ROUND – AND ROUND …
FLYING THROUGH AIR!
OOOOOOOOOOOOOA!
WHOOOOOOOOOOOOOOOOOOOO

8pm

Yes. I think the kraken remembers me.

Yuck. There's kraken-snot everywhere.

Even inside my pockets! Uh-oh, it's coming

for me again. Quick!

8.02pm

Phew, in the tunnel at the end of the

creature room.

Boris! Where are you?

Oh. That. Chicken.

Oh. That. *Smell.* There's another blast of

it!

Calling Boris's name in a whisper. The

last thing I want to do is be caught by—

YEOOOOWWWWWWWWWW!

8.09pm

Oh dear. Oh. Very. Dear.

Have now been very much nipped on the bottom by a Giant DeathClaw Lobster! Won't be able to sit down for a week!

Captain Chomp heard me yell, dragged me into another room and imprisoned me before I had chance to explain.

My secret mission is over. I'm locked in a lobster pot. I've lost my chicken.

I haven't found the Golden Eyepatch
and now a Giant DeathClaw Lobster has
scuttled off with Boris's fake beard. Fair
to say it's not going well. Better face facts.
My chance to be in the movie, to prove
myself to the other pirates, is over.

ALL IS

INDEED

LOST.

Captain Chomp has gone after the
lobster. They are having a tug-of-war over
the beard.

Argh! Another blast of that awful smell!
Wait, I see where it's coming from . . .
There's a tank over there with a shark in it.
Just before the smell wafts, all these bubbles
appear in the water.

I know what it is!! A ROTTEN-SEA-
CABBAGE-EATING STINKER SHARK.
No wonder Jolly said, "May the rotten-
sea-cabbage-eating Stinker Shark never
pass wind in your direction!" That smell
drowns out everything!

Oh dear. Captain Chomp has lost the battle with the lobster. It's scuttling off with Captain Chomp chasing after it. It's taking the beard back to one of the lobster pots.

What is the matter with that lobster?! It's always scuttling off with things: Boris's button, the microphone, my hat . . . Maybe it likes collecting things, like Boris collects gold and—

GOLD! THE GOLDEN EYEPATCH TROPHY! THAT'S IT! I WONDER IF . . . I BET . . . OF COURSE!

I must get out of this lobster pot!

BORIS!

Don't care how loud I yell now. I NEED MY CHICKEN!

BORIS!

I can see something coming down the tunnel in the gloom. An odd shape . . . Wait, I'd recognise that bonnet anywhere. It's Boris!

Come on, Boris, karate-chop the lobster pot! Get me out!

It's worked – I'm free! (So glad I sent Boris for karate lessons and not ballet.) Quick, no time to lose. FOLLOW THAT BEARD!

Captain Chomp spins round and sees us. He's trying to grab Boris – wait! She's doing karate moves in the air. He's backing away . . . Boris is sniffing the air and getting excited. I knew it! She can finally smell the gold of the Eyepatch! She's darting into the lobster pot . . .

Ooh, she's darted out again, chased by the lobster, holding the beard in its claw.

Another epic battle begins. Go, Boris! Chicken is winning!

No, lobster is winning!

No, beard is winning!

No, chicken is winning!

No, chicken is laying egg. Oh. That.
Chicken!

Lobster is winning! Ooh, it's nipping
at the Bonnet of Ridicule. Think it wants
that too. Don't suppose Boris will like that
much.

Yeek!

No, apparently not!

Lobster looks like it's regretting arguing
with a bonnet-wearing, karate-chopping
chicken.

It's hidden the beard back inside the
pot – and come out again! It's going for
Captain Chomp's bottom now. Think it's
going to need more yoga sessions . . .

Boris is flapping and squawking and

darting inside the lobster pot. She's coming

out – she's got the—

BEARD?! FOCUS, BORIS!
GO BACK!

She's gone back in . . . She's coming out . . .

With her rainbow beret?! So THAT'S

where it went to! Oh. That. Lobster!

Boris is going in again. And . . .

Oh. My hat. Thanks very much. She's going back! And . . . she's done it! She's got Jolly's Golden Eyepatch trophy in her beak!

Once she was close enough, she could smell it above those dreadful farts from the rotten-sea-cabbage-eating Stinker Shark!

Captain Chomp is just staring in shock, with a lobster dangling from his bottom. His face has gone the colour of Redruth's hair! He looks more embarrassed than Jolly when he was de-haired by the StuffHunter™. He can't have known the trophy was there. Oh, for a camera!

I think, if we ask nicely, Captain Chomp might just row us back to go and see Jolly. After all, it was his lobster that stole the Golden Eyepatch!

Come on, my brilliant chicken, let's—

What? OK, you can keep wearing the bonnet. What? OK, and the beard. Now let's— Seriously? Oh, OK, AND you can keep hold of the trophy for now! Just don't tell Jolly.

8.50pm

We arrived at the Barrel Theatre (remains

of) with Captain Chomp and his lobster.

Jolly was up on stage, surrounded by a

television crew. He was clutching a skull,

just like he did in that Sharkspear play.

(Made him look extra dramatic. Wow, he's

good.)

"Alas, poor Eyepatch! I lost it, Horatio ..."

he said to the cameraman.

I thought we should just tiptoe down

the front, without drawing attention to

ourselves. Yeah, right! Boris "The-not-at-

all-crazy" Chicken ran for the stage with

the trophy in her beak, charged at Jolly

(making him drop the skull in surprise),

laid an egg, then karate-chopped it. What a mess. I tiptoed on stage to get Boris back before she tried to attack the skull. Jolly looked at me in amazement. This is how it went:

JOLLY: Oh, how I have longed for this most blessed moment! The return of my beloved Golden Eyepatch! Joy of a thousand joys! But, dear hearts, is this a chicken I see before me?!

ME: Um . . .

JOLLY: And Tentacles Wonderbeard! How in the name of William Sharkspear did you get off the

Rather Big Rock Where We Put Naughty People We are Really Fed Up With?

ME: Um . . .

JOLLY: And why is this bird the bearer of my Golden Eyepatch trophy?

ME: Um . . .

JOLLY: Explain yourself, boy! Speak now or may the singing of a thousand out-of-tune mermaids really get on your nerves!

ME: The lobster took it! Boris tried to sniff the gold—

JOLLY: Sniff the what?

ME: She's part-dragon.

JOLLY: Part WHAT?

ME: But there was a really smelly fart—

JOLLY: Your chicken did a smelly fart?

ME: No, Captain Chomp—

JOLLY: Captain Chomp did a smelly fart?

ME: No, Captain Chomp had a Stinker Shark and THAT did the smelly fart, so Boris couldn't smell the gold.

JOLLY: And your chicken is part-dragon.

ME: Yes. But we tracked the lobster down to its hideout and

THEN Boris could smell the gold.
So she started karate-chopping
the lobster—

JOLLY: Because your part-
dragon, gold-sniffing chicken
also does karate.

ME: Yes.

pause

JOLLY: What an unusual bird.

ME: That's one way of putting
it.

JOLLY: And the reason she's
wearing a bonnet and a beard?

ME: Probably better not to ask.

There was a stunned silence. Everyone was staring at me. I gulped. Jolly was staring at me. Then staring at Boris. Then at Captain Chomp at the back of the theatre (remains of), who was holding his wretched DeathClaw Lobster and grinning sheepishly.

I took the trophy out of Boris's beak, wiped off the slobber and gave it back to Jolly. I smiled my best don't-shout-at-me-see-how-nice-I-am smile . . .

Then Jolly laughed and laughed! He clutched the trophy in his fist and lifted it high above his head. All the pirates in the theatre began to clap and cheer. Boris took a bow.

"You know," Jolly whispered to me. "It might be rather interesting to make a film about that bird."

Then Jolly bellowed to the audience:
"Once more unto the film set, dear friends,
once more!"

The pirates all cheered again and Jolly
clapped me on the shoulder. "You've got
the part back. And as for this remarkable
bird? Who cares that she's a chicken?
What's in a name . . .? A finer Carrot
the 'Parrot' the world will never see!

To hair and make-up, me hearties! Swiftly now! And may the snot of a pepper-fed kraken never drip in your porridge!"

Hmm. Now there's an idea . . .

SEPTEMBER 6TH

Sitting on set, in our movie-star chairs, waiting to be called up in front of the cameras.

Have just bought two ice creams from the ice-cream boat, which Jolly sent for us to celebrate the return of his Golden Eyepatch. Mint chocolate chip for me and vanilla for Boris, with some Chick-O-Snacks on top.

Blackbeard looks really fed up. Probably doesn't help that his porridge must have been revolting this morning after I snuck in some kraken-snot! Haha. Revenge is sweet! Or, in this case, revenge is snot.

Ooh! *Pirate Monthly* have just asked if they can feature me and Boris in their next issue.

Everything is perfect. We'll be famous.

I really do have the

Best.

Chicken.

Ever.

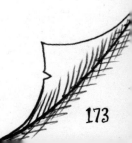

OCTOBER 10TH

No time to write any more! Busy filming

☺

DECEMBER 31ST

No New Year's resolutions. I'll think about that next year . . . Too busy being famous.

Boris and I are starring in a real, proper movie! I'm creating some inventions to help. This is going to be great!

What could possibly go wrong?